# Johnny Lion's Rubber Boots

An I Can Read Book™

# Johnny Lion's Rubber Boots

by Edith Thacher Hurd
Pictures by Clement Hurd

HarperCollins*Publishers*

HarperCollins®, 📖®, and I Can Read Book® are
trademarks of HarperCollins Publishers Inc.

Johnny Lion's Rubber Boots
Text copyright © 1972 by Edith Thacher Hurd. Copyright © renewed 2000 by Thacher Hurd.
Illustrations copyright © 1972 by Clement 'Hurd. Copyright © renewed 2000 by Thacher Hurd.
Printed in the U.S.A. All rights reserved.
www.harperchildrens.com

Library of Congress Cataloging-in-Publication Data
Hurd, Edith Thacher.
    Johnny Lion's rubber boots / by Edith Thacher Hurd ; pictures by Clement Hurd.
        p.      cm. — (An I can read book)
    Summary: Until his father brings him some rubber boots, a young lion searches for ways
to entertain himself on a rainy day.
    ISBN 0-06-029337-3 — ISBN 0-06-029338-1 (lib. bdg.) — ISBN 0-06-444295-0 (pbk.)
    [1. Lions—Fiction.   2. Animals—Infancy—Fiction.   3. Rain and rainfall—Fiction.
4. Play—Fiction.   5. Boots—Fiction.]   I. Hurd, Clement, ill.   II. Title.   III. Series.
PZ7.H956 Js   2001                                                                          00-32026
[E]—dc21

1   2   3   4   5   6   7   8   9   10
❖
New edition, 2001

*to Abigail Brooks*
*of*
*The Peaceable Kingdom*

It was raining.

Drip, drip, drip.

7

"Oh dear," said Johnny Lion.

"It is raining.

I cannot go out to play."

"Yes," said Mother Lion.

"It is raining too hard.

You cannot go out to play."

"But I have a big rain hat

and a big raincoat,"

said Johnny Lion.

"But you do not have any

rubber boots,"

said Mother Lion.

"Oh dear, oh dear.

What can I do?" said Johnny Lion.

But Mother Lion

did not hear Johnny Lion.

She was busy.

"What can I do?" said Johnny Lion.

He went upstairs.

He went downstairs.

Then he hid in a dark, dark closet.

"BOO!"

said Johnny Lion.

But Mother Lion was very, very busy.

"Don't be silly, Johnny Lion,"

said Mother Lion.

"Go upstairs and play."

So Johnny Lion went upstairs to play.

15

He made a lot of things.

Little things.

Big things.

And then he knocked them down.
Crash!

Crash!

CRASH!

But Mother Lion was busy.

She did not hear

the crash, crash, crash.

"Oh dear, oh dear," said Johnny Lion.

"I wish I could

go out and play."

But Johnny Lion saw that everything

was wet.

The rain went

drip, drip, drip.

Then Johnny Lion painted

a big picture.

He painted a picture

of a little tiny hunter.

He drew wild animals.

He drew wild people.

He drew a picture of a big, big
SCAREY THING.

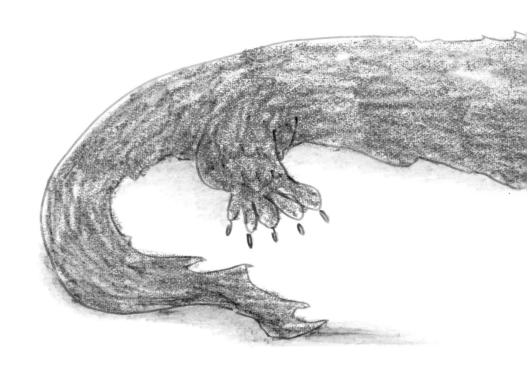

"GRR-grr-grr,"

went the big SCAREY THING.

"I love little hunters."

But the little hunter

did not see

the big SCAREY THING.

24

The big SCAREY THING
went creep,

creep,

CREEP!

The big SCAREY THING
went jump,

jump,

JUMP!

But the little hunter

climbed a tree.

Just in time!

Then he waved his tail.

He went "Grr-grr-grr!"

WHOOSH!

Away went the big SCAREY THING.

Then Johnny Lion

took his paintbrush.

He took his red paint,

and he painted his tail all red.

"Oh, oh, oh," yelled Johnny Lion.

"The great big SCAREY THING

bit me in the tail."

The red paint went

drip, drip, drip

all the way down the stairs.

"What a mess," cried Mother Lion.
"Johnny Lion, clean up
all that awful mess."
So Johnny Lion cleaned up
all that awful mess.

Then Johnny Lion built

a dark, dark cave.

He built a cave with:

a big box,

two chairs,

and a blanket.

Johnny Lion got inside his cave.

He growled, "Grr-grr-grr!"

He howled, "OO-OO-OO!"

Then Mother Lion came upstairs.

She was not scared a bit.

"What a mess," she said.

"Johnny Lion, clean up your room."

So Johnny Lion cleaned up his room.

Then he looked outside.

"It is not raining now," he said.

"Please may I go out to play?

Please, please, please?"

"Not now," said Mother Lion.

"Everything is very wet,

and you do not have any

rubber boots."

Poor Johnny Lion.

He did not know what to do.

He sang a little song,

just to himself.

He sang a very, very little song.

"Rainy day.

Rainy day.

Go away.

Go away.

Let the sun come out to stay.

Rainy day.

Rainy day."

36

Johnny Lion stopped singing.

Someone was coming.

It was Father Lion.

Father Lion had something.

"What is that?" said Johnny Lion.

"It is something for you,"

said Father Lion.

"Oh," said Johnny Lion.

"Just what I wanted,

red rubber boots."

"Yes," said Father Lion.

"I thought so."

Johnny Lion put on

his red rubber boots.

40

"Just right," he said.

"Now may I go out to play?"

"Yes," said Mother Lion.

"Put on your red rain hat

and your red raincoat,

and don't get wet."

"Of course not," said Johnny Lion.

Then he went outside to play.

Everything was wet.

Everything was dripping.

Drip, drip, drip.

There were lots and lots of puddles.

Johnny Lion walked
in all the puddles.
He walked in his new
red rubber boots.

Johnny Lion jumped in the puddles.

"You will get your feet all wet,"

called Mother Lion.

But Johnny Lion

did not hear Mother Lion.

He was very busy.

Then Johnny Lion saw

a big yellow dog.

"Oh, oh, oh," cried Mother Lion.

"Look out, look out, Johnny Lion."

Johnny Lion climbed a tree.

He waved his tail.

He growled, "Grr-grr-grr."

Zip-zip-zip.

Zippity-zippity-zippity—zip!

Away went the big yellow dog.

"I was not scared a bit,"

said Johnny Lion.

Johnny Lion

sat up in the big wet tree.

He looked down

on the big wet world.

48

Then it began to rain again.

Drip, drip, drip,

on the tree.

Drip, drip, drip,

on Johnny Lion's rain hat.

Johnny Lion climbed down

out of the tree.

He got inside of a great big box.

The rain went

drip, drip, drip.

Mother Lion looked for Johnny Lion.

"Oh, oh, oh," said Mother Lion.

"Where is Johnny Lion?"

Mother looked.

Father looked.

"Oh, oh, oh," cried Mother Lion.

"That big yellow dog

got my little Johnny Lion."

"Nonsense," said Father Lion.

Then Mother Lion put on her raincoat.

She put on her rain hat
and her rain boots.

Father Lion took his big umbrella,

and they went to look for

Johnny Lion.

Mother and Father Lion

looked and looked.

"Johnny Lion, Johnny Lion,"

called Mother Lion.

"Johnny Lion, come here at once,"

said Father Lion.

Just then they heard a noise.

It was a growling noise.

"Growl, growl, growl."

Then they heard a howling noise.

"Howl, howl, howl."

"Oh," said Mother Lion.

"The big yellow dog has Johnny Lion
in that box!"

"Oh no he hasn't,"

someone said.

Johnny Lion jumped out.

"Oh," said Mother Lion.

"The big yellow dog

did not get you after all."

"Of course not," Johnny Lion said.

Then Father Lion held
his big umbrella over Johnny Lion.
And Mother Lion gave Johnny Lion
a great big hug.

"Now come inside," said Mother Lion.

"Do I have to come inside?"

said Johnny Lion.

"Yes," said Father Lion.

"You are very, very wet."

"Not my feet," said Johnny Lion.

And he was right.

He took off his new red rubber boots

and his feet were just as

dry as dry could be.

"Mother Lion,

put the kettle on,"

said Father Lion,

"and we will all have tea."

So Mother Lion put the kettle on.

And they all had tea.